The Twelve Dancing Princesses

Look for all the
SCHOLASTIC JUNIOR CLASSICS

SCHOLASTIC JUNIOR CLASSICS

The Twelve Dancing Princesses

Adapted by
Ellen Miles

SCHOLASTIC INC.

New York   Toronto   London   Auckland   Sydney
Mexico City   New Delhi   Hong Kong   Buenos Aires

Copyright © 2003 by Ellen Miles.

All rights reserved. Published by Scholastic Inc.
SCHOLASTIC and associated logos are trademarks and/or
registered trademarks of Scholastic Inc.

ISBN 0-439-45708-4

12 11 10 9 8   12 13 14 15 16/0
                Printed in the U.S.A.   40
            First printing, January 2003

For Leda

Contents

The Twelve Dancing Princesses

Chapter 1

Jessamine

JESSAMINE yawned.

Her mouth opened so wide that a ruby-throated hummingbird with gold-spangled wings nearly darted right into it.

Jessamine barely noticed. She rubbed her eyes and yawned again. The garden was full of pleasures, but she was really too sleepy to enjoy it properly. She would have loved to sniff each fragrant lily in turn, wander down the enticing path of mossy green stones that led to a sparkling waterfall, or sit on the carved wooden swing beneath the huge spreading oak tree and pump her legs until she was flying high above the world.

But she was just too, too sleepy.

And the garden was so huge. Even if she weren't sleepy, it would take forever to explore. Why, it could take a whole day just to walk from the rose bowers to the sunflower maze! It took a small army of master gardeners, head gardeners, under-gardeners, and gardener's boys to do all the pruning and trimming and mowing and mulching and weeding. Now and again, Jessamine's father would spend an afternoon picking off dead pansy blossoms or fertilizing the lilacs, since he loved nothing better than gardening. But for the most part, he was forced to leave such chores to the gardeners, because he was much too busy with affairs of state.

For, you see, Jessamine's father was the king.

Which made her a princess.

And she was sleepy because, as is so often the case with princesses, she was under a spell. Jessamine truly loved to dance, loved it better than anything. But because

2

of the spell, she danced all night every night, and never got enough sleep.

Perhaps the story should really begin like this:

Once upon a time, in a land far away, there lived a young girl named Jessamine. She was extraordinarily beautiful, so beautiful that when she walked in her father's garden, the birds flew down to circle around her head for a closer look and the flowers turned their heads to watch her go by. Jessamine was the youngest of twelve sisters, and it was said that each of the twelve princesses was more lovely than the last, no matter which order you took them in.

The king and queen had named their girls after the flowers they so loved, starting with Azalea, the eldest, and on through Buttercup, Calendula, Daisy, Daffodil, and Dahlia (the triplets), Echinacea, Forsythia, Gardenia, Heliotrope, Iris, and, of course, Jessamine. Jessamine's sisters all had golden hair, ranging from a glowing honey color (Azalea) to flaxen (Echinacea), but Jessamine's hair was as dark and shining as a raven's wing.

Besides being lovely, the princesses were charming and kind and well bred and intelligent (well, except for the triplets, who were really rather silly), and the king adored them. He adored each of them and all of them, not just as a father adores his daughters and not just as a king dotes on his heirs, but as a very sad man clings to his only consolation.

The princesses were just as lovely and charming and kind and well bred and intelligent as their mother, the queen. The king and queen had always been happy with each other and content to be surrounded by their lovely daughters, until the last one, Jessamine, was born. During her birth, the queen died and, from that moment on, the king lived only for his flowers and his daughters.

4

Unfortunately, he did not spend nearly as much time with his daughters as he might have wished.

For Jessamine was not the only princess who was sleepy. All twelve sisters were always tired. They rarely rose from their beds before ten, and then they yawned and drooped over their lunch, too weary to admire the golden plates and jewel-studded goblets from which they ate and drank. They napped through the afternoon, dozed into the evening, and barely roused themselves for a late supper before heading back to their room. All of this sleepiness was on account of two things: a passion that made them want to dance, and a spell that made them unable to stop.

The princesses had identical beds, all in a row in one long, narrow room in the west wing of the palace. The room's only windows were narrow and higher than any person could reach. The walls were hung all around with rich, bright tapestries, picturing wondrous animals at play in fanciful landscapes. The princesses' mattresses were of the finest swansdown, their sheets were of the smoothest spun silk, and their blankets were of the softest velvet. But the princesses' beds were hardly used at night.

Oh, they went to bed. They changed into snowy-white nightdresses, kissed their dear father good night, and slipped between the sheets. Then the king would step outside their room, close the massive wooden door, and lock it up tight with the large brass key he kept around his neck.

There was only one key that fit the massive brass lock in the massive wooden door, and the king never let it out of his sight. Yet, night after night, the princesses managed to slip out of their room and dance for hours, until their satin slippers were quite worn through.

Every night, their father kissed his daughters and bade them to sleep well. Every night, they slipped into their beds.

And every morning, their ladies-in-waiting presented twelve pairs of worn-out dancing slippers to the king.

As you can imagine, the shoemakers in the kingdom were not unhappy. They had all the business they could want, making pair after pair of lovely satin slippers for the princesses.

But the king was very unhappy indeed. And he issued two royal decrees: First, he banned dancing in his kingdom, for dancing had brought him only unhappiness. Second, he declared that if any man could discover how it was that his daughters wore out their shoes night after night, that man could choose one of the daughters to be his wife. And when the king stepped down from the throne, that man would be the next king.

Any man could try, whether peasant, nobleman, or prince. And a number of men *had* tried. They had arrived full of hope and confidence. They had been welcomed by the king and his court and given a sumptuous meal. Afterward, they had been locked in the long, narrow room in which the princesses slept. And in the morning? They had disappeared. Every last one of them, never to be seen again. Nine suitors had tried so far, and nine had disappeared.

And so, the king was still unhappy.

Jessamine hated to see him so sad. But she loved to dance, and she just *had* to dance, night after night, even though it broke her father's heart. She never even tried to tell him where and why she and her sisters danced, for she had no words to explain it. Nor did she want to give up dancing. She did not know it was a spell that kept her from telling. All she knew was that she had danced away every night that she could recall, every night since she was old enough to walk. Jessamine was now nearly sixteen years old, and she could not remember ever feeling quite fully awake during the day.

Chapter 2

Julian

JULIAN stretched.

He flung his arms up to the sky and smiled up at the sun. It was a good day, with puffy white clouds sailing above and plenty of green, green grass for his charges, the cows, to graze on. He whistled and waved to his friend Michael, who was just coming to the pasture, walking up the path behind three cocoa-brown cows.

Julian was a strong, handsome young man with clear blue eyes and dark curls. He lived in a tiny village in a far corner of the kingdom, where he herded cows for the kindly farmer who had taken him in when he was orphaned at an early age.

Julian was fond of the farmer and his

wife, and he was grateful for all they had done for him. He liked working outside all day and he loved the gentle cows with their velvety brown eyes. He had a comfortable bed to sleep in, plenty to eat, and clothes to cover his back. It should have been enough for a poor, orphaned peasant boy.

But Julian was a dreamer. He dreamed of bright palaces and glowing tapestries, blooming gardens and fine horses with bridles of silver and gold. When he was small, Julian had heard tales of knights and their ladies, kings and queens, and princesses with lovely faces and silken gowns. He had never forgotten those stories. Someday, he thought, someday he would see all that. Someday, he might even marry a princess.

The townsfolk teased Julian for his fancies. How would a cowherd meet a princess? A cowherd drove his cows to pasture every morning and brought them back every evening, and that was his life.

If Julian was lucky, he would meet a nice peasant girl, someone who didn't mind the smell of cows. They would marry and have a small farm of their own. That was enough to hope for. Dreaming of anything else was just plain foolish.

On that day in early spring, when the apple trees were just sending out their tender green buds and tiny yellow flowers carpeted the pastures, Julian heard for the first time about the twelve dancing princesses. Michael was full of news, for he had just come back from a fair in a nearby village where he had heard talk of strange places and people. He told Julian of the king's promise to reward anyone who could solve the mystery of the worn-out shoes. "This is your chance!" said Michael, laughing. "All you have to do is follow those princesses, and you'll end up a king in a palace after all!"

Michael was joking, of course. Even though the king had said any man could try, nobody would expect a cowherd to arrive at the palace hoping to marry a princess.

But from that moment on, Julian could think of nothing else.

Three days later, the farmer looked up from his midday meal to see Julian herding the cows back from the pasture, whistling as he walked. "What are you doing home so early?" the farmer asked.

"I'm leaving," Julian said simply, handing over the switch he used to prod the cows along. He thanked the farmer for all he'd done for him. Then he gathered up his clothes into a bundle and set off, ignoring the laughter of the townsfolk as he strode through the village for the very last time.

Chapter 3

A Gift

JULIAN walked along the dusty road, carrying all his worldly belongings. At first, he enjoyed the journey. He had never before traveled beyond the village of his birth, and everything he passed was new and interesting. He saw birds he'd never seen before, rivers that flowed faster than any he'd dreamed of, and forests so dark and deep he could not imagine how any person or animal could find a way through them.

By the fifth day, though, Julian was hungry and tired. He had long ago finished off the meager provisions he had brought along. His shoes, already worn when he began the journey, were full of holes. And his body was stiff and sore after four nights of sleeping on the cold ground.

On the outskirts of a village quite a bit larger than his own, Julian stopped near a shallow stream to rinse his face and hands. If he were more presentable, perhaps he might convince a tavern owner to put him to work in exchange for some food.

He was splashing water over his head when he heard a cry. "Get out of there, you stubborn fool!"

Was someone talking to him? It was true that he could be stubborn when he wanted something, but how could this stranger know that? Julian peered up at the far bank of the stream. There he saw a woman waving her hands and shouting at a large fawn-colored cow that was trampling a well-tended garden.

Julian waded across the stream and climbed up the bank, wiping his dripping hands on his trousers. "May I help you?"

he asked the woman. "I know a thing or two about cows."

She looked at him gratefully. "Would you? My neighbor says that if he catches her in his garden one more time, she'll be his. I depend on the milk she gives, even though she is the devil to keep."

The woman was not young, but Julian could see that she had once been very beautiful. Her eyes were a deep violet, just like the star-shaped flowers he'd seen along the roadside. She held herself straight and tall, and while her gown and cloak were patched and faded, they were clean. When she smiled, her eyes seemed to twinkle and shine just as the water in the stream did when the sun danced on it.

Julian smiled back. "Which way is your home?" he asked.

The woman pointed to a small cottage, nearly hidden by a colorful overgrown garden. There was a small fenced area next to it. "She belongs behind that fence," she said, nodding toward the cow. "But the gate is broken, and she finds her way out."

Julian broke a small switch from a nearby sapling. Then he pursed his lips and made a noise to catch the cow's attention. When she swung her head around to see him, he dashed behind her and gave her a tap on the hindquarters. The cow started to walk toward the little cottage, and the woman ran ahead to open the gate. Julian stayed behind, herding her along.

Once the cow was safely behind the fence, Julian swung the gate closed and examined its lock. Sure enough, it was hanging loose. Using a strip of leather from his bundle, he tied it up securely. "That should hold her," he said, reaching over the fence to give the cow an affectionate pat.

The woman was grateful, and she offered him some bread and cheese. While they ate, Julian told her of the reason for his journey. He thought he saw her eyes darken when she heard he hoped to discover the secret of the dancing princesses, but she said nothing.

As he was preparing to leave, she disappeared for a moment, then returned carrying two tiny trees in one hand. In the other she held a small golden rake, a little golden pail, and a silken towel, as white as snow. Julian was astonished. Where had this poor woman found such things?

She did not explain, but said only this: "The palace grounds begin just past these woods. When you arrive, find a place on the grounds where you can plant these two laurel trees. Rake them with the rake, water them from the pail, and dry them with the towel. They will grow more quickly than you can imagine, and when they are the same height as you, say this to them: 'My little laurel trees, with my golden rake I have raked you, from my golden pail I have watered you, with my silken towel I have dried you.' Then you may ask the laurels for whatever your heart desires, and they will give it to you. Only remember this: You must never tell a soul about how the laurels have helped you. If you do, all that they have helped you attain will disappear."

Julian vowed to keep the laurels' secret and accepted the trees and the tools. He wondered if the woman were mad, for what she had told him seemed beyond common sense. But at the same time, there was something in her eyes that made him believe that what she had said might be true. Julian thanked her, packed everything into his bundle, and started off again toward the palace.

He wondered if he would know it when he saw it. As it turned out, there was no question. The palace, white and gleaming, rose from the surrounding countryside the way a shining mountain rises from the plain. The grounds surrounding the palace were carefully tended, with every tree, stream, and path placed for the most pleasing effect. Julian wandered through the grounds until he came to the palace gardens, which were beyond his wildest imaginings. He had never seen such colors, nor smelled such intoxicating fragrances. Shimmering peacocks strutted the rolling lawns, their feathers reflecting every color of the rainbow as their tails unfurled like enormous fans. Birdsong filled the air and butterflies darted about, catching Julian's eye as they sipped from each flower in turn.

"Have you come for a job, then?" A man approached Julian, smiling and nodding at him. "You've arrived at just the right moment. We need a new gardener's boy to care for our bouquet garden." The man looked Julian up and down. "Once we get you into some clean clothes, I think your looks will please the princesses."

Everything happened so fast that Julian's head was spinning, but he did not forget to plant the laurel trees the woman had given him. That very evening, he dug two holes near a fountain, planted the trees, gave them plenty of water and a good raking, and wiped them down with the silken towel.

By the following morning, the trees had already grown to reach Julian's waist. After tending to them, he went to the bouquet garden and picked enough flowers for twelve small bouquets, as the master gardener had instructed him to do. Then he waited near a bower at the west side of the palace, dressed in his clean green gardener's tunic.

The sun was high in the sky before the princesses appeared, drifting into the garden in twos and threes. Julian listened and watched as they came, learning their names as he heard them address one another with teasing and laughter. Azalea and Buttercup came first, barely acknowledging

Julian as he handed them their bouquets. Calendula nodded as she took hers, and Daisy, Daffodil, and Dahlia broke into giggles. Echinacea and Forsythia were too busy talking about their new gowns to even notice the new gardener's boy, while Gardenia, Heliotrope, and Iris just yawned and rubbed their eyes as they accepted their flowers.

Jessamine looked straight into Julian's eyes.

He felt a little shock go through him as her gaze met his. The princesses were more beautiful than he ever could have imagined, but he thought Jessamine was the most enchanting of them all. He could not look at her for more than a second or two before he found himself blushing and looking down at his feet. She was not like any other girl he had ever seen. She was like a creature from some other world, far beyond his own.

Jessamine waited patiently until Julian

remembered to hand her the last bouquet. Then she smiled. Smiling, she was even more beautiful. Julian's heart pounded so hard he thought it might burst.

He remembered Michael laughing as he suggested that Julian might try his hand at winning one of the princesses for his wife. Now he, too, saw how ridiculous that was. He would tend his laurel trees, pick his twelve bouquets each day, and try to be content now that he had at least *seen* a princess. With time, perhaps he would be able to forget that he had ever dreamed of marrying one.

Chapter 4

New Gowns

JESSAMINE looked down at her bouquet, admiring the sweet violets, the fragrant lilies of the valley, the perfect pink tulips. She buried her nose in the flowers and took a long, happy sniff.

She glanced back at the young man who had handed them to her, noticing sleepily how odd it was that his cheeks turned pink the moment he saw her looking at him. She thought his cheeks looked rather nice, flushed that way. In fact, he was quite handsome. Much more handsome than any of the men who had come to spy on her and her sisters, hoping to find out their secret so they could marry a princess.

Another one was due to arrive that night.

He was a prince from a very wealthy kingdom far to the south. Jessamine yawned. And then, out of the corner of her eye, she caught the gardener's boy stealing a glance at her. He was standing where she'd left him, stock-still in his gardener's clogs and tunic. Jessamine felt a little shock go through her as her eyes met his for the second time that morning. She could not seem to manage to look away.

"Jessamine!" She felt a tug at her sleeve. "What are you gaping at? Haven't you heard me calling you? Come along, now. It's time for the final fitting of our new gowns." Azalea didn't even wait for an answer. She strolled up the path, back toward the palace, expecting Jessamine — and all the other sisters — to follow her.

And they did. It wasn't often that any of them disobeyed Azalea.

Daisy, Daffodil, and Dahlia hurried to catch up with Jessamine. "Did you see the way that gardener's boy looked at you?" asked Daffodil.

"Did you see?" Dahlia echoed.

"The gardener's boy!" Daisy repeated. "He was looking at you!"

All three of them giggled until they were gasping for breath.

Jessamine tossed her hair. "I don't know what you're talking about," she said.

"He was," said Heliotrope, who was walking along beside her, carrying her own bouquet of narcissus and pansies. "I saw it, too."

Jessamine yawned. It was a pretend yawn this time. "My, I'm sleepy," she said, in order to change the subject.

Six of the seven sisters nearby yawned, too. Even a pretend yawn can be contagious.

They continued to yawn throughout the fitting of their new gowns. The royal seamstress began to yawn as well, as she pinned their hems and checked the stitching on the princesses' dresses.

The new gowns were lovely. Azalea's was a deep red, while Buttercup's was a soft, velvety brown. Calendula's gown was of shimmering gold, and the three triplets were lovelier than ever in cobalt blue. There was a pale green dress for Echinacea, dove gray for Forsythia, and ivory-white for Gardenia. Heliotrope's tawny hair was set off perfectly by her gown of dark green, while the pink gown Iris wore flattered her pale skin. Jessamine thought they were all very nice gowns, but secretly she believed that hers was the most glorious. It was the deep bluish-purple of the evening sky. She would wear her diamond necklace and tiara with it, and the diamonds would look like the first stars that peek out after the sun has set. She could hardly wait to see how the gown moved and swirled when she danced in it.

The princesses wore the new gowns to

dinner that night, which pleased the king. It also pleased the prince who had come to try his luck at learning the secret of the worn-out slippers. He bowed deeply as the princesses, led by Azalea, filed into the dining room, their long, full skirts rustling as they moved. Jessamine, at the end of the line, took her seat next to her father at the head of the table. The prince sat at the other end of the table, Dahlia on his left and Echinacea on his right.

He was a handsome, broad-shouldered man, with a strong, hawklike face. His manners were perfect, his conversation polite. He seemed especially interested in everything Heliotrope had to say, and she, in turn, paid him every attention.

When the last golden platter had been cleared and the final drops of wine had been sipped from the jeweled goblets, the king pushed back his high-backed silver chair and announced that it was time for bed. He led the princesses and the prince to the long, narrow room in the west wing. The king shook the prince's hand and wished him the best of luck. "If you can tell me where my daughters go at night and how they get there, I will be pleased beyond all measure," he told him. "You will be welcome to everything I own, and I will be proud to have you as a son-in-law."

Jessamine saw the prince's eyes search out Heliotrope's. Then he looked back at the king and nodded. "I will do my best, Your Majesty," he said. A servant showed him to his bed, which was behind a folding screen at the far end of the room. The princesses took turns kissing their father good night, Azalea first and Jessamine last. Then the king stepped out of the room and locked the door.

When he unlocked it in the morning, all twelve princesses were there, but the prince was not. And at the end of each bed was a pair of dancing slippers, full of holes and quite worn through.

Chapter 5

Invisible

WITHIN an hour, everyone on the palace grounds had heard about the worn-out slippers and the disappearing prince. "It's a shame," the master gardener said to Julian, shaking his head. "He was a fine young man, from all I heard."

Julian caught a glimpse of the king that morning, when His Majesty took a stroll in the apple orchard. The king barely seemed to notice the trees surrounding him, which were bursting with pink-and-white blossoms that perfumed all the surrounding air with the sweet fresh smell of springtime. He strolled up and down the rows of trees, his hands behind his back and his head drooping to his chest. The only time he even glanced up was when he heard the sound of his daughters' voices.

Julian heard them, too, and realized that he must rush to finish making his bouquets. He had made Jessamine's first that day, choosing the finest blossoms and arranging and rearranging them until he felt sure they were perfect. He added one more rose from the garden, a large yellow bloom whose fragrance almost made him dizzy. Then he hurried to put together eleven more bunches of posies. He picked red tulips and blue forget-me-nots, pink peonies and purple snapdragons, white daisies and yellow lilies. He bundled them into eleven charming bouquets, accenting each with a sprig of apple blossom and some fragrant lilies of the valley. Then he ran to the bower to meet the princesses and deliver their flowers.

Most of the princesses ignored him again, but the triplets giggled harder than ever when he handed them their bouquets, bowing slightly from the waist as the master gardener had taught him. Dahlia's eyes went to the bouquet he had made for Jessamine.

"Ooh," she said. "I like *that* one. It's the prettiest by far. May I have it instead of this one?"

Julian turned pale and began to stutter. "I — I —" How could he say no to a princess?

But the triplets just glanced at one another and broke into gales of laughter, then strolled off holding the bouquets he had given them.

Jessamine lagged a little behind her sisters, so that she was by herself when she came through the bower. This morning, she was wearing a dress of shimmering yellow silk, exactly the color of the lilies Julian had been picking. He was glad he had included several in her bouquet. He handed it to her, bowing a little more deeply in order to avoid meeting her eyes.

31

But she waited for him to straighten before she took the flowers, and their eyes met anyway. Julian felt the same jolt he'd felt the day before.

Jessamine smiled, nodded, and strolled away slowly, sniffing her flowers.

Julian watched her go. He thought of how very beautiful she was, and of the kindness and intelligence in her eyes. Suddenly, he knew he must try to win her hand.

But how?

Julian finished his duties, then went to the fountain to care for his laurel trees. To his amazement, they had grown even more overnight, so that they were both now as tall as he was. Their leaves were dark green and shining with health. Julian raked the soil around the trees, then watered them thoroughly. Then he wiped them with the silken towel. As he worked, he thought and thought.

Finally, when he was finished, he looked

around to see if anyone was watching. Feeling rather foolish, he faced the trees and spoke. "My little laurels," he said, "with my golden rake I have raked you, from my golden pail I have watered you, with my silken towel I have dried you." He stopped for a moment, wondering if he really could ask for anything he wanted. Then he took a deep breath and went on. "Teach me how to become invisible," he finished.

At that very instant, a pure white flower bloomed on a branch of one of the trees. Hesitantly, Julian reached out and plucked it. He sniffed it, but it had very little fragrance. He looked it over, wondering what he was meant to do with it. Then, shrugging, he tucked it into the buttonhole in his collar.

And suddenly, his collar wasn't there. Nor was his hand, nor his arm, nor — any part of him. Julian gasped. The flower had made him invisible!

He plucked the white blossom back out of his buttonhole, and saw his hand reappear. He put it back, and disappeared once more. "Ha!" he cried. It was the most peculiar and amazing thing he had ever seen.

Next, with the flower in his buttonhole, he reached out and touched the little golden watering can. It did not disappear. Then he picked it up — and it was gone! He did the same with the rake, and the towel. He touched a nearby tree. It did not disappear. But when he broke off a branch, the branch disappeared immediately in his grasp.

It was wonderful. Julian spent the next hours experimenting with his new power. Then, while standing invisibly next to two servants outside the main gate of the palace, he heard that another hopeful suitor had arrived that day.

Julian made up his mind. This was his chance! With the help of the flower, he could find out once and for all where the princesses danced at night and what became of the men who tried to follow them. He lost no time. When the servants went back into the palace, an invisible Julian followed them. He was soon lost in a baffling maze of corridors and doorways. By a stroke of luck, he managed to find himself in the dining hall just as the princesses, the king, and the latest suitor sat down to their evening meal.

At first, Julian found it nearly impossible to take his eyes off Jessamine, who was wearing an elegant gown of deep green velvet, nearly the same color as the leaves of the laurel trees. He stood as near to her as possible, choking back a sneeze at one point that would have been sure to give him away. When he finally began to look around, Julian was awed by the beauty of the room. The richly woven hangings, the enormous wooden table, the high-backed chairs. He'd never seen anything like it! And when the food began to arrive, borne on golden platters by servants dressed in gold-trimmed red velvet uniforms, Julian's mouth began to water. The smells wafting toward him were unlike any he had smelled before. He could not resist stealing a small bit of meat from a servant who walked right past him, bearing a platter. It was still heaped with food even after the noble folk had taken all they wanted. The meat was savory and delicious, one of the finest things Julian had ever tasted.

The meal did not last long, as the princesses were tired as usual and the suitor was exhausted from his travels. Before the clock struck eight, Julian found himself following the princesses, the king, and the suitor to the long, narrow room in the west wing of the palace.

Chapter 6

Who's There?

JESSAMINE woke with a start. As usual, she'd allowed herself to fall asleep, luxuriating in the delicious softness and warmth of her bed. But, also as usual, her precious rest was not to last longer than a few minutes.

Nine of her sisters were already awake, lighting candles, making their beds, and bustling about in their closets. They chattered gaily, excited as always about going to the dance. Only Jessamine, Heliotrope, and Calendula, always the three last to get up, were still dozing.

"Come, Jessamine," said Azalea, leaning over her bed. "It's time to be stirring."

Jessamine moaned. "Five more minutes?" she pleaded. As much as she loved dancing, she loved the thought of sleeping a few more minutes even more, right that moment.

Azalea snorted. "And be late for the dancing? Don't be silly. Up, up!" She pulled Jessamine's covers off and handed her a robe. Then she went off down the row to rouse Heliotrope and Calendula.

Jessamine stumbled over to her closet and pulled out a dress of ruby-red silk. She rummaged around until she found her petticoats, her leggings, her under-clothes, and a brand-new pair of satin slip-pers, the same red as the dress. Yawning, she brought everything over to her bed and tossed it down in a great, untidy pile.

Azalea, walking by after waking the last two slugabeds, gave her a frown. "You must learn to take better care of your things, Jessamine," she said. "Remember, you're not a —"

"Not a peasant," Jessamine finished. "I

know. How could I ever forget? I live in this enormous palace, I am waited on by dozens of servants, I eat delicacies like quail eggs and oysters on a daily basis, and I have a closet full of gowns in every color of the rainbow. I dance the night away, each and every night. How many peasants live like that? I know, I'm a princess. But sometimes, just sometimes, I envy the peasants who are left to sleep in peace."

Azalea just rolled her eyes and stalked away. Jessamine shrugged. She glanced over to the screen, behind which the latest suitor was probably asleep. Lucky him!

Or not. Maybe he wasn't all that lucky, since it was almost certain that after this night he would never again be seen in the kingdom. Too bad. He was as handsome as the rest of the suitors, and possibly quite a bit more interesting. Jessamine had heard him talking with her father at dinner that night, something about a new way to build a drawbridge. She had followed the discussion and even joined in with some of her own ideas, until she was distracted by a sound behind her. It was a sound just exactly like someone swallowing a sneeze. She'd looked around, but nobody was there. Still, she'd felt as if there were some sort of presence, hovering near her in the dining hall.

In fact, that same feeling came over her now. She had finished pulling her dress over her head and was beginning to lace up her shoes when she felt it. Like someone nearby, watching.

"What is it, Jessamine?" asked Heliotrope, as she passed by carrying a fresh pair of white gloves. "You look as if you'd seen a ghost."

"Not a ghost, exactly," Jessamine answered, "and not *seen*, exactly. But there's something . . ."

"Oh, stop dawdling, you two!" called Azalea from across the room. "It's time to put on our tiaras and be off."

40

She was loud enough to wake the suitor, who stuck his head around the screen. Rubbing his eyes, first in tiredness and then in disbelief, he stared at the twelve princesses, all dressed in their finest gowns and gleaming with sparkling jewelry. They were probably quite a sight, thought Jessamine, looking around at her sisters. But that was no excuse for staring.

Ignoring him, Jessamine went to her dressing table and chose a tiara of white gold encrusted with amethysts and pearls. She perched it on her head and turned to face Azalea. "I'm ready," she said. Now that she was up and dressed, she could hardly wait to dance. And yet — she couldn't help feeling that something was odd that night. "But, Azalea?"

"What now?" Azalea, impatient to go, had her hands on her hips.

Jessamine wasn't sure how to explain what she was feeling. She was almost positive that the suitor was not the only watcher in the room. But Azalea would never listen, anyway. "Oh, nothing," she said finally.

Azalea nodded. "Right, then." She clapped her hands, and Jessamine and her sisters lined up eagerly. Their gowns were perfect, their jewels sparkling in the candlelight, their white-gloved hands clutching the bouquets the gardener's boy had given them that morning, their slippers nicely laced. They were ready to dance. "Shall we go?" She bent to pull aside a small carpet, intricately woven in black and red. Then she reached out, took hold of a big iron ring set into the floorboards, and pulled.

A trapdoor opened to reveal a set of stone stairs receding into the darkest dark imaginable. Without hesitation, Azalea picked up a lantern, hitched her skirt, and led the way.

Down, down the stairs they went. The suitor, having hurried into his clothes, managed to work his way into the line between Echinacea and Forsythia. Then came Gardenia, Heliotrope, and Iris, who carried another lantern. Its light was almost immediately sucked up by the great darkness surrounding them, but the princesses stepped nimbly down the stairs in their satin slippers, as surefooted as mountain goats. They probably could have found their way with no lanterns at all, thought Jessamine, after all the nights they'd come down these stairs. She yawned, stopping for a brief moment to adjust her tiara.

When she started down the stairs again, something held her back.

She gasped.

Something was pulling on her gown! "I'm caught!" she cried out, as she pulled back, hoping her gown would come free. "Someone has stepped on my gown! Someone is following us! Our secret will be discovered! We'll never dance again!"

Azalea's voice drifted back from the

front of the line. "Jessamine, must you be such a silly goose? Hold the lantern high, Iris, so your sister can see that there is nobody there. Your gown must have caught on a nail."

Just then, Jessamine's gown came free. She clutched her skirts around her and moved off quickly, her heart beating so fast she thought it would jump out of her chest. The strange feeling she'd had since she awoke was even stronger now. And she was *not* a silly goose. She knew perfectly well that there were no nails in a stone step.

Chapter 7

To the Ball

JULIAN cursed himself silently. How could he be so clumsy? The flower in his buttonhole made him invisible, but it surely did not make him graceful. It was so dark that he could not see his own feet, but that was no excuse. He should have noticed Jessamine slowing down, and stopped in time to avoid stepping on her dress. Idiot!

But there was no time to waste in lecturing himself. If he did not keep up, he'd soon be lost on these dark, dark stairs. Treading very carefully, he followed as close behind Jessamine as he dared.

The stairs seemed to go on forever. Down, down, down they went. Just when

Julian thought it wasn't possible for the dark around him to be any darker, it was. The lamp Iris held was like a distant star, a pinprick in the velvety darkness.

Then, slowly, it began to grow lighter. The stairs ended and Julian found himself walking across a flat, open area, dimly lit by an odd, greenish glow.

The princesses moved along even more quickly now, and Julian had to hurry to keep up. The greenish glow turned brighter until Julian could see even Azalea at the head of the line. She came to what looked like a long row of bushes, a hedge that made an impenetrable fence. Stopping only briefly at a tall wooden door, she reached out to open the latch. The door swung open and Azalea stepped through it, followed by each of her sisters, the suitor, and finally, an invisible Julian.

He had to stifle a gasp when he saw the forest they now walked through. Every leaf on every tree was spangled with drops

46

of silver, shining and glittering in the greenish light. Julian looked around with wonder, thinking he had never seen anything so lovely. No birds flitted through these trees, no animals scurried beneath. The wood was silent and still.

Beyond the silver forest was something even more spectacular: a grove of trees whose leaves were dusted with lustrous gold, all glowing warmly in the faint light. The princesses did not even seem to notice the beauty as they hurried through the gilded forest, though Julian noticed the suitor gazing about.

But there was something even more amazing still to come: the third forest, in which every tree was covered with dazzling diamonds. The leaves were dripping with them. Diamonds! They took every bit of the dim light and threw it all around, reflecting and magnifying it so that Julian's eyes nearly hurt with the brightness of it all. He wanted to slow down and take it all in so he could remember this amazing sight for as long as he lived. But the princesses did not tarry in the diamond-strewn wood. They hurried on, and Julian followed them.

They came next to a large, dark lake, with tiny wavelets lapping at its shore. There at the edge of the lake were twelve small rowboats decorated with pretty pennants. Next to all but two of the boats stood ten tall, handsome men dressed in the finest garments. They bowed deeply as the princesses approached and helped the ten eldest into the boats. The new suitor seemed to know what was expected of him: He took Iris's hand and led her to the eleventh boat. Jessamine stepped carefully into the remaining boat and picked up the oars. Quickly, Julian stepped into the boat with her. A tiny frown flashed across her face as she felt the boat move under his weight, but she said nothing.

The boats moved off, slipping nearly

silently through the dark water. Nobody spoke. The men rowed quietly as the older princesses took off their gloves and trailed their pale hands in the water. The boat Julian rode in lagged behind a bit, and he heard Jessamine mutter something about how her boat seemed so much slower and heavier that night.

Julian watched for the far shore, curious about their final destination. Suddenly, there it was: a palace carved out of black rock, ablaze with the light of a thousand lanterns. It loomed above the lake, twinned by its reflection in the still, dark water. Sprightly music poured from the castle, a welcoming sound indeed in that dark, greenish quiet.

The boats landed at a long stone pier, and the men sprang out to tie them up and give their hands to their princesses. Jessamine tied her own boat and hurried along behind the couples who rushed toward the palace, their expectant faces lit by its glow. Julian followed Jessamine, keeping close behind her as she slipped through the massive gates, into the courtyard, and up the stairs to the huge wooden doors that were flung open, spilling out music and light.

The princesses and their escorts slipped inside, with Jessamine and an unseen Julian right behind them.

Julian was dazzled. This palace was far more sumptuous than the palace of Jessamine's father. Rich hangings covered the walls, with gilt-edged mirrors hung between to best reflect the glowing tapestries. Every surface held an enormous bouquet of flowers: deep bright blossoms Julian had never seen before. A black marble floor, studded with diamonds and rubies, shone beneath his feet, while tall columns of gold held canopies of bloodred satin overhead. A small orchestra of musicians sat playing golden instruments on a raised stage at one end of the cavernous room.

50

While Julian stood gaping, the princesses began to dance. The eleven escorts moved effortlessly, twirling first one partner then another so that no princess ever stood still for more than a heartbeat. The music swirled around the dancers, spurring them on as they darted and wove about the floor, creating ever-changing patterns that left Julian feeling slightly dizzy.

The princesses danced beautifully, their faces alight with pleasure in the music and the movement. They never stopped, not even to catch a breath or take a sip of wine. They danced and danced, their swirling skirts just grazing the floor, their satin slippers moving in perfect time. It was as if they had to dance, had to *keep* dancing, as if dancing were their greatest joy. Julian thought that Jessamine was the best dancer of the twelve. He watched her smiling face and he knew there was no question. She loved dancing, loved it better than anything else in the world.

Chapter 8

And Home Again

THOUGH the music filled her head and kept her feet moving, Jessamine was unable to rid herself of the feeling that someone unseen was watching. She danced and danced, twirling from one handsome young man to another. She barely noticed when one tune ended and another began, so distracted was she by that strange feeling.

In every other way, this night was like every other night she could remember. First there was the trip down the stairs, through the bejeweled forests, and across the lake. Then there was the dancing. Hours of it! Waltzes and minuets, allemandes and gavottes and quadrilles. What joy! When the clock struck three, the music would stop and it would be time to eat. The food was always delicious and the wines were the finest, and Jessamine was often hungry after all the dancing.

After dozens of dances, Jessamine was beginning to tire. She began thinking about bed as she whirled in the arms of a tall, blond man in a soldier's uniform. She imagined the embrace of her blankets instead, the softness of her sheets instead of the rough feel of the soldier's wool tunic. She imagined kicking off her dancing slippers, which were already worn quite through in at least five places, and resting her tired feet on her swansdown mattress.

Just then, the clock struck three. The music stopped, and Jessamine and the soldier stopped, too. Bowing, he offered one arm to her and the other to Daffodil, who was standing nearby. The three of them walked through a large arched opening at the end of the ballroom and into a long, narrow dining hall. The only furnishings in the room were a long, narrow table covered in a golden velvet cloth and twenty-five stately golden chairs, twelve up each side and one, much taller than the others, at the head. The tableware was even finer than that in Jessamine's father's palace, with goblets of crystal edged in gold and platters of gold edged with sparkling jewels. The only light in the room came from three enormous golden candelabras set on the table, one near each end and one in the middle. Each held dozens of tall white candles, whose flickering yellow light danced off the jewels and precious metals of the table settings.

Jessamine slipped into her place, opposite an empty chair. Her sisters each took a place opposite one of the dancing men, Iris facing the newest suitor. He looked a bit baffled and a little lost. It had been quite a night for him already.

He'll get used to it, thought Jessamine. She picked up a bejeweled fork and moved it this way and that, admiring the way the gems sparkled in the candlelight.

There was a flourish of trumpets, and with a majestic sweep of an ebony fur cape, a tall, imposing woman entered the room. Her eyes, the color of a stormy sky at twilight, flashed as she glanced around the room. She gave a slight nod of approval as her gaze passed over Iris's suitor, who had leaped to his feet along with the other men.

"Sit," she said, holding up her hands. "Welcome to my table, friends. Eat, drink, take pleasure in the food and wine I offer you."

This was Lady Esmerelda, their hostess. At first, Jessamine remembered, it had been just the lady and the princesses at that long table. Then, one by one, the suitors began to arrive, and each night, the princesses danced longer than before. Once the suitors ate the food and drank the wine, they never left.

Lady Esmerelda smiled a thin, crafty

smile as she took her seat at the end of the table. "Yesss," she hissed, as if to herself. "Now there are eleven." She gestured to a servant, who held a large carafe of ruby-red wine. "Let us drink a toast to our new arrival," she said.

The servant filled each glass, then stepped back into the shadows.

Lady Esmerelda held her glass high and saluted Iris's suitor. "Welcome, sir!" she said. "With your coming, we are now nearly complete. Before long, one more of your kind will arrive. And when he does, the dancing will never stop!" She let out a short, strange giggle, and Jessamine felt a little chill go down her spine.

She felt something else, as well. That presence again. This time, she felt as if someone were sitting in the empty seat across from her. She almost expected a hand to lift the empty wineglass at that spot, joining in the toast.

But that was ridiculous, of course. Jessamine gave her head a little shake and lifted her own glass, looking over it into the eyes of the newest suitor. He had a sudden, trapped look, like a rabbit caught in a snare. *Don't drink!* Jessamine almost said it aloud, but stopped herself. Oh, what did it matter? They all drank. And they all seemed perfectly happy afterward, perfectly content to dance their lives away. After all, who did not love to dance?

The man took a tiny sip of wine, then another, longer drink. Almost immediately, the frightened look in his eyes disappeared. He gazed up the table at Lady Esmerelda and lifted his goblet high. "To our most lovely and welcoming hostess!" he declaimed.

"Hear, hear!" all the men chorused, lifting their goblets in her direction.

The men and the princesses ate and drank their fill. Then the clock struck four, and it was time to go. Back to the boats they went, for the long row across the dark lake. Again, Jessamine's boat felt heavier than usual, but she decided she was just tired. At the opposite shore, the men — including Iris's suitor — bowed and took their leave, rowing back to the palace.

As Jessamine walked through the diamond wood, she began to think again of her bed. In the gold wood, she pictured herself curled up beneath her soft, warm quilt. And then, as she walked through the silver wood, her thoughts were interrupted by a loud, sudden crack just behind her.

"What was that?" she asked, stopping in her tracks.

Up front, Azalea was all impatience. "Come, Jessamine. Our beds are waiting! It was only the sound of drums from the palace." She began to walk more quickly, and Jessamine had little choice but to hurry along as well. But she knew very well that Azalea was wrong. Those were not drums she had heard.

Chapter 9

The Spell

HE should have resisted. Julian knew it was dangerous to break off a branch of silver-spangled leaves. But somehow, he just *had* to. How else could he ever be sure that he had seen all he had seen? The jeweled woods, the black lake, the fabulous palace, the dancing, the banquet, the imposing Lady Esmerelda and the way her eyes, somehow so familiar to him, had held the men at the table spellbound — his head was whirling. Most of all, he pictured how content Jessamine had looked, spinning around the room as if she'd been born to dance. He'd never seen her happier.

Julian knew he had better bring something back, something that would prove that he had not simply been dreaming an amazing dream.

When Jessamine stopped walking in the silver wood, Julian stopped as well, closing his hand around the little branch he'd snapped off so that it would be as invisible as he was. She glanced back, but of course she saw nothing. Julian noted the alarm and worry in her eyes, and felt remorseful. Somehow, he must let her know that she had nothing to fear. But he had no time to think about that now. He had to hurry to keep up as the princesses rushed back to their room, back to their beds for a precious hour or two of sleep. Back up the stairs they climbed, their weary feet treading heavily on the massive stone steps. After climbing for what seemed like forever through the thick darkness, Julian saw light from above as Azalea opened the trapdoor. And finally, he followed Jessamine back into the long, narrow room with twelve waiting beds.

The exhausted princesses kicked off their shoes and fell into bed without even changing their clothes. Julian curled up near the door, hoping to catch a brief nap before he must begin his day's duties.

Then the first cocks crowed and the door swung open. Julian saw the king standing outside as a chambermaid slipped into the room. The king waited, a hopeful look on his face, as the maid reached for the pair of slippers at the bed nearest the door, Azalea's. She picked them up and tiptoed back to the open door. When she showed the worn shoes to the king, his face fell. Slowly, he turned and walked away.

Julian slipped out the door and went the other way down the corridor, turning right and left and right again until he found his way to an outer doorway. He went straight to the gardener's shed and put on his green tunic. Then he took the white laurel flower out of his buttonhole and reappeared, tired but ready for a day's work. Before he picked up his tools, he looked down at the sprig of silvery leaves he still held. In daylight, it shone even brighter, with a glow like the full moon's on a clear night. He slipped the branch into the pocket of his tunic and went off to make twelve bouquets, even though the princesses would not appear for hours.

The nosegays were ready and Julian was arranging them in a basket when the master gardener appeared. "Boy," he said, "I have an errand for you. At the edge of the palace grounds lives the Lady Mirabelle, who knows more about plants than anyone in the kingdom. The king's roses are ailing, and I must know how to cure them. Bring her this leaf," here he held out a leaf to Julian, "and ask her what is wrong."

Julian looked at the leaf, which was covered in black spots. Surely, the roses would die if a cure was not found quickly. He nodded to the master gardener. "I'll be back in time to give the princesses their bouquets," he promised. He left the basket in the shade and trotted off, tired but glad to have an important errand.

It was a radiant morning, and Julian enjoyed his trip through the palace grounds and into the deep wood just past them. His mind wandered as he trotted along, remembering all he'd seen the night before.

He could not have been more surprised when, following the master gardener's directions, he arrived at the cottage of the woman whose cow he had driven home, the woman who had given him the laurels. He found her sitting outside, sorting some dried herbs.

"We meet again," she said, smiling as he approached. When Julian looked into her eyes, he stopped in his tracks.

She saw his reaction. "Ah," she said quietly. "So you have made the acquaintance of my sister, Esmerelda."

Julian nodded wordlessly. Of course! Those violet eyes. So unusual. Now he knew where he'd seen them before. But the Lady Mirabelle's knowing eyes were as kind and soft as the Lady Esmerelda's were cruel and hard.

"You must keep your distance from her," advised the lady. "She is bitter and sad and very, very dangerous. No man has yet returned to this world after drinking her wine. And you see how the princesses must return, night after night. Those girls do love to dance, but she has twisted that love into a duty."

"But why —" Julian began.

Lady Mirabelle sat down and patted the bench beside her. "When Esmerelda and I were very young," she began, "the king was also young, and we knew him well. We went to every ball at the palace. He was merely a prince then, of course. Esmerelda was certain that she was destined to marry him and become queen. He was fond of both of us, but in the end he shocked everyone by marrying the gar-

64

dener's daughter." Julian gasped, and she nodded. "None of the princesses know that their mother was ever anything but noble." She smiled. "Esmerelda and I have certain — powers," she went on. "I chose to turn my attention to plants and healing. Esmerelda — well, she was so angry and hurt that she vowed revenge upon the king. She has spent her days since then trying to take all happiness from him. If she has her way, his daughters will spend their lives at her palace, dancing eternally with the men she's enchanted with her wine. Of course, the princesses are enchanted by the wine as well. Otherwise they would never break their father's heart this way."

Julian nodded. The king was very sad now, and he could only imagine how inconsolable he would be if Lady Esmerelda's words came true and the princesses stayed in her palace forever, dancing their lives away.

But what could he do? If he tried his luck as a suitor, he would likely spend all the rest of his days dancing in that strange, far-off palace. If he told the king what he had seen, he would have to reveal the secret of the laurels, and he could not do that.

Julian remembered that he must return to the palace in time to give out his bouquets. He showed the rose leaf to Lady Mirabelle, and she gave him an herbal tincture to apply to the plants. When he bid her farewell, she looked deep into his eyes. "Please," she said, "promise me you will stay away from my sister."

Julian looked down. "I cannot," he said. He knew he would follow Jessamine and her sisters again, no matter how dangerous the Lady Esmerelda might be. "But I thank you for the warning." And he ran as fast as he could back to the palace grounds.

Chapter 10

The Silver Branch

JESSAMINE stretched and yawned and rubbed her eyes. She barely felt rested, but her sisters were up and bustling about and she knew she must rouse herself to do the same. Their father would be disappointed if they did not at least join him for lunch. As it was, he breakfasted by himself every day, alone at the great dining table with only the silently waiting servants for company.

She chose a simple beige linen gown from her wardrobe and slipped it on, yawning some more.

Once all twelve princesses were dressed, Azalea led them out of their room and down the corridors. One by one, they walked out of the grand doors of the west wing. That new gardener's boy was waiting for them, dressed in his green tunic and holding his basket of bouquets. He gave a slight bow as he handed flowers to each sister in turn, blushing only slightly this time when the triplets broke into giggles as they accepted theirs. When Jessamine's turn came, he handed her the last bouquet without meeting her eyes. She accepted it and looked down into the blooms, wondering what special blossom he had added this time. Her eyes widened when she saw a sprig of silver-spangled leaves tucked into the very center of a bunch of white narcissus.

Jessamine gasped. She stared at the gardener's boy, willing him to meet her eyes. Finally, he looked up at her. The expression in his clear blue eyes was impossible to read.

What was she to make of this? Somehow, this young man had discovered their secret. Was he going to tell? Would she never again dance the night away? Jessamine swayed a little, feeling a bit faint. He couldn't tell! He mustn't! If he did, it would mean the end of dancing.

"Are you all right?" Iris asked, turning to stare at her.

"Fine," Jessamine managed to say. "I'm fine."

"Then come along," Azalea ordered. "Father is waiting for us in the dining room."

Iris took Jessamine's arm. "You're probably just hungry," she said, leading her along the path beneath the honeysuckle bower. Jessamine glanced back once at the gardener's boy and found that he was gazing after her, still wearing that mysterious expression.

Jessamine puzzled over it all day long, but as usual she was far too tired to make much sense of anything. She moved automatically through the afternoon, eating just enough at lunch to keep her father from worrying. She joined him afterward for a stroll through the pear orchard, which was just coming into bloom.

That night, Azalea did not have to nag at her to get out of bed when the time came to dress for the ball. Jessamine rose quickly, feeling once again that sensation of being watched. It stayed with her all through the trip down the stairs and through the silver wood, the gold wood, and the diamond wood. Once again, she felt that her boat was especially slow, and once again she felt that someone observed her as she danced until her slippers were worn through.

She sat at Lady Esmerelda's table, hardly listening to the murmur of conversation, hardly noticing the delicious food she picked at. Through it all, she felt that presence.

Her boat felt low in the water on the return trip, and this time she was not so ready to blame its slowness on her exhaustion. The walk through the diamond wood was as usual, but when they entered the wood of golden leaves, Jessamine heard a loud crack behind her and her heart leaped into her throat.

"What was that?" Azalea asked this time. She had heard the sound all the way at the head of the line.

This time, Jessamine provided the answer. "It was nothing," she told her eldest sister. "Just the sound of drums from the palace."

Chapter 11

The Branch of Gold

JULIAN was exhausted. Two nights in a row he had followed the princesses, and the day before he'd had to run the errand to Lady Mirabelle's on top of his normal duties. He could barely see straight as he made up the bouquets. Still, he chose as carefully as always when it came to creating Jessamine's. He mixed wild yellow celandine with white irises and added three tulips that were so deeply purple they were almost black.

And in the very center, he tucked the sprig of golden leaves.

He didn't know why he did it. Somehow, he wanted Jessamine to know that he knew her secret. He wanted her to know it was safe with him. She and her sisters would not have to give up the dancing they so loved, not on his account. Spell or no spell, Jessamine would hate him forever if she could never dance again because of him. And even if he could figure out how to do it without telling the secret of the laurels, he would not tell the king just to win her hand. He was too proud for that. He would not marry someone who did not choose to marry him, someone who had been given to him as a prize. He would not do it, no matter how beautiful she was, no matter how many years he had dreamed of marrying a princess.

Julian realized it was getting late. It was nearly time to greet the princesses. He straightened his tunic, combed his hair with his fingers, and set off with his basket of bouquets.

His heart began to beat fast when he caught the first glimpse of Azalea, coming down the path toward him. As usual, she took her bouquet graciously yet without actually seeming to *see* him. He bowed as he handed out the rest of the bouquets, one by one. His heart was truly pounding by the time the triplets appeared. He saw Daffodil's glance linger on the bouquet with the purple tulips, but he ignored the merry look in her eyes and managed to keep from blushing when she whispered, "For Jessamine?"

Echinacea, Forsythia, and Gardenia, all passed by and accepted their flowers. Then came Heliotrope, and a little bit behind her, Iris. Julian could hardly bring himself to look down the path to see whether Jessamine was coming. She must be, she *must*! What if she picked this day to lie abed, or to gather her own bouquet?

Iris was already far down the path, bouquet in hand, by the time Jessamine came walking slowly along. Had she lingered on purpose, so as to be alone with him? Julian felt his heart swell with hope.

She came closer, closer. She was wearing a soft pink gown, the color of apple blossoms just before they open. Her cheeks were flushed slightly, the very same pink, and her eyes were bright. She looked more beautiful than ever. Julian reached into his basket, picked up the bouquet he'd made for her, and offered it with a bow.

He did not — *could* not — watch as she examined it. But he heard her gasp when she saw the spray of golden leaves. "How . . . ?" she began, but he shook his head before she could even finish the question, raising his eyes to meet hers.

"I cannot tell you," he said.

"But will you tell my father our secret?" She looked fearful. He knew she could not bear to think of never dancing again. And — terrible thought! — perhaps she could not bear the thought of being forced to marry him.

"No."

She looked at him suspiciously. "Then

what do you want from me?" She pulled a heavy purse from an inside pocket and held it out to him awkwardly. "If it's money you want, here it is. There's plenty more, if you'll keep your silence."

Julian did not even glance at the purse. He bowed stiffly to Jessamine, turned, and walked away down the path.

Chapter 12

Diamonds

WHY had she done that? Jessamine felt awful as she watched the gardener's boy walk away, his back held stiff and straight. She'd obviously insulted him. But she didn't understand. If he wasn't going to tell her father, did that mean he didn't want to marry one of the princesses? That he didn't want to marry *her*? If that were so, then why was he following them? For clearly, that's what he was doing. The silver branch had made her wonder, and the gold branch was almost certain proof. If it wasn't because he wanted to be king someday, then *why*? She'd thought maybe he wanted to be bribed to keep the princesses' secret. But plainly, that wasn't it.

Oh, if only she weren't so *sleepy*, perhaps she could understand. Yawning, Jessamine wandered down the path toward lunch. She was already looking forward to her afternoon nap.

For the next two days and nights, nothing happened. That is, all the *usual* things happened: meals and naps and strolls in the garden during the day and dancing and feasting all night long. But no new suitors appeared to try their luck, and Jessamine heard no strange noises as she and her sisters made their way to and from Lady Esmerelda's palace. Most notably, her bouquets — while charming — did not include sprays of gold- or silver-dusted leaves. Nor did the gardener's boy meet her eyes as he offered Jessamine her flowers.

Jessamine tried to convince herself that she had dreamed the whole thing. But a quick check under her pillow each night revealed the branches she'd saved from her bouquets. There was no doubting that the gardener's boy had followed her and her sisters and watched them dance. Perhaps he had done it just to satisfy his curiosity and would never do it again. Perhaps the sisters' secret was safe, after all. Jessamine hoped so. Her sisters would be furious if they knew they'd been spied on in such a way.

Then, on the third night, Jessamine heard something. It happened just as the sisters were making their way back through the diamond-strewn wood. Crack! There it was again, that sound. Her voice trembled a little as she assured her sisters that it was, once again, the sound of drums.

When she went back to bed, she did not fall asleep, even though she was just as exhausted as she always was after a night of dancing. Instead, she lay staring at the ceiling and waiting for the first light of dawn to find its way through the high, narrow windows. She lay there and thought, wondering what she was going to do if there was a branch of diamonds in her bouquet that morning.

Dawn came, but of course none of the sisters stirred for several hours after that. Jessamine heard the door creak open and saw the chambermaid come in to check on Azalea's shoes. She heard the roosters crow and the sound of birds singing their hearts out.

Finally, Azalea rose, stretched, and began to dress. Jessamine leaped out of bed and was ready before any of the others. Azalea was bewildered, but Daffodil, Daisy, and Dahlia were not. "She can't wait to see that gardener's boy," Jessamine heard Daisy whisper to Dahlia, who giggled and passed it on to Daffodil.

"Yes, she'll marry him and then spend her days dressed in a tunic, with muddy knees and twigs in her hair," Daffodil whispered back.

Jessamine pretended not to hear. She

waited as patiently as she could until her sisters were ready, then followed them out to the gate where the gardener's boy waited, his flower-filled basket at his side. She hung back as her sisters received their bouquets, then came forward to accept her own.

There were lilies in it, and bluebells, and a great fragrant stem of purple lilac.

And there was a spray of diamonds.

Jessamine gasped. "It *was* you!" she said to the boy.

He didn't speak.

She narrowed her eyes. "Do you still intend to keep our secret?"

He nodded. "I promise."

"Jessamine!" called Azalea. "Come along! What are you doing?" She reappeared, along with Jessamine's other sisters.

"She's talking to that handsome gardener's boy," Dahlia said.

"I think she wants to marry him!" Daffodil said, laughing.

"What shall I wear to the wedding?" asked Daisy, joining in the fun. "Perhaps a tunic just like his?"

Jessamine knew she was blushing. How could her sisters tease her like that, right in front of the boy? But when she turned to give him an apologetic look, he was gone.

She turned back to face Azalea. Her face must have shown how distressed she was, for Azalea asked her what was wrong.

Jessamine could not help herself. She told her older sister everything, showing her the diamond branch for proof.

"How dare he?" Azalea asked. "I'll call the guards this minute and have him thrown in the dungeon. That will ensure that he keeps our secret."

"No!" cried Jessamine.

"No?" asked Azalea, giving her a curious look. "What shall we do with him, then?"

"Let's tell the rest. We can decide together." Somehow, Jessamine could not bear the thought of the gardener's boy, with his clear blue eyes, rotting in the dungeon.

So they gathered all the sisters in the rose garden, and Jessamine told the story once more, of how the gardener's boy had followed them and learned their secret. Forsythia and Gardenia were horrified and agreed with Azalea that he should be imprisoned immediately. Echinacea was not so sure, nor were Buttercup and Calendula. Daisy, Daffodil, and Dahlia were serious for once when they heard the tale, and Heliotrope and Iris sat on either side of Jessamine, stroking her hair in a comforting way as they all talked it over.

In the end, it was silly Daisy who came up with the idea. "He's handsome enough," she said. "Why not take him with us to Lady Esmerelda's? He'll make a good dancing partner."

Chapter 13

Julian's Fate

AS it happened, Julian had overheard the entire discussion. Slipping a laurel flower into his buttonhole, he had followed the princesses into the rose garden and listened to their debate.

He was not at all surprised by Daisy's idea. In fact, he had come to the same conclusion himself. It was the only solution. He would present himself to the king as a suitor, go with the princesses to Lady Esmerelda's palace, and drink his hostess's wine. If that meant he stayed in that strange underworld forever, dancing for eternity with Jessamine, well, there could be worse fates. He was willing to sacrifice himself for Jessamine's happiness. He was very sorry that the king would lose his daughters and he wished there were some way to avoid that. But he couldn't think of any.

He wandered away from the rose garden, deep in thought, and soon found himself near his laurel trees. He took the white flower out of his buttonhole and reappeared. He looked down at his green tunic in dismay. It was clean and presentable — for a gardener's boy. But if he were about to present himself as a suitor, he had to do better. He thought about it as he raked, watered, and dried his two trees. When he was done, he spoke to them. "My beautiful laurels," he said, "with my golden rake I have raked you, from my golden pail I have watered you, with my silken towel I have dried you." He took a breath. "Dress me like a prince."

A pink flower appeared on one of the trees. Julian reached out to pick it. Holding it, he closed his eyes for a moment, then opened them again and looked down at himself. He gave a shout of amazement when he saw how he was dressed, in a black velvet suit with a sky-blue silk shirt beneath and a matching black velvet cap. His feet were shod in the finest shoes he'd ever seen, much less worn: soft black leather with silver buckles. Julian ran to the fountain and tried to catch a glimpse of his reflection in the rippling water. The young man looking back at him smiled gravely and nodded in a princely way.

Julian stuck the pink flower in his velvet buttonhole, straightened his velvet cap, and set off for the main gates of the palace. He was greeted there by the king's men, who bowed and welcomed him. They ushered him inside and escorted him to the dining hall, where dinner was just about to begin.

Julian was not at all sure how a prince should behave. He bowed to the king when he was introduced, avoiding the man's sad eyes. He answered the king's questions carefully, trying to conceal his true background without exactly lying. Fortunately, when the king noticed the laurel blossom in Julian's buttonhole, the conversation switched to plants and flowers and everything else was forgotten. The king seemed impressed with Julian's knowledge of gardening, and the two conversed companionably until the princesses arrived and dinner was served.

Julian was sorry that he was too nervous to enjoy or really even taste the delicious food that was presented to him. It all looked and smelled so wonderful! But he felt Jessamine's eyes on him all through the meal, and every sip of wine he took reminded him of the wine he would be drinking at another palace, very soon.

Before he knew it, the meal was over. The king rose, and Julian and all the princesses rose as well. The king led them all out of the room and through the torch-lit corridors until they came to the long, narrow room with twelve beds — and a thirteenth behind the screen. Bidding Julian good night and wishing him good luck, the king then kissed each of his daughters in turn and left the room, locking the door behind him.

Julian lay on his bed behind the screen, much too nervous to even think about sleeping. After his three nights of following the princesses invisibly, he knew exactly what to expect. Sure enough, it wasn't long before he heard the sisters bustling about, giggling and chattering as always. He sat up on his bed and waited until he was sure they were dressed, then peeked around the screen to see Azalea opening the trapdoor.

Just as he had on the other nights, Julian fell into line behind Jessamine and followed the princesses down the long, dark stone stairway and through the forest of gold, the forest of silver, and the forest of diamonds. He saw Jessamine glance back at him as they passed through the woods, but the expression in her eyes was hard to read.

When they arrived at the dark lake, eleven suitors and twelve boats were waiting. Julian stepped in and offered Jessamine his hand, helping her in as well. He took the oars. "May I?" he asked, and she nodded, so Julian rowed them both across the lake.

The palace came into view, its lanterns casting a glow upon the dark water. Jessamine helped Julian tie up the boat, and they walked together, at the end of a line of couples, into Lady Esmerelda's palace.

The music was already playing as they entered the ballroom. Julian had always enjoyed dancing, and now he took Jessamine in his arms and whirled her off across the black marble floor. The princesses and their suitors danced for hours, switching partners so that Julian danced with each sister in turn. They seemed to like him; he overheard Forsythia whispering to Buttercup that she had never imagined a gardener's boy could dance so well. And even Azalea seemed impressed with his fine manners.

When the clock struck three and the musicians struck up the last tune of the night, Julian found himself dancing with Jessamine again. He loved the way she floated across the floor in his arms, glancing up at him now and then as the music swirled around them.

Then the music ended. It was time for the feast. Following the other couples, Julian escorted Jessamine into the dining hall and took his seat in the chair opposite hers. Moments later, he rose to his feet as Lady Esmerelda appeared, sweeping into the room. She glanced around at the twelve full chairs and smiled a victorious smile.

She took her seat and gestured to a servant, who stepped forward to fill each guest's goblet with wine. When the goblets were all full, she lifted her own and looked down the table at Julian. "Let us toast our new arrival," she said. "Welcome, sir!" Her eyes held Julian's, and he found their violet color mesmerizing.

Feeling as if he were dreaming, Julian reached out to pick up his goblet of wine. But just as he raised it to his lips, Jessamine leaped up. "Don't drink!" she cried, dashing the goblet from his hand. "I would rather marry a gardener!"

Chapter 14

Jessamine and Julian

JULIAN sat stunned, but only for a moment. Then he rose to his feet and went around the table to take Jessamine's hand.

At the same moment, each of the other suitors went to take the hand of the princess opposite him.

The spell was broken.

Lady Esmerelda sat speechless, her mouth a thin line of disappointment. Then, abruptly, she rose and stalked out of the room.

As one, the twelve couples also stood and walked out of the dining hall, each pair gazing into each other's eyes as they strolled out of the palace and down to the pier. Before long, twelve small boats were making their way across the lake, and laughter echoed across the dark water.

"Look!" said Julian, pointing back toward the palace. Jessamine turned to see. As she watched, the thousand lanterns that lit Lady Esmerelda's palace winked out, one by one, until the entire building disappeared into the darkness.

"We'll never dance there again," Jessamine said softly.

Julian thought she sounded sad. "You can dance at your own palace now," he said.

"And so I shall," Jessamine answered, smiling at him.

And so she did. The very next day, the king declared an end to his edict forbidding dancing and invited everyone in the kingdom to come to a ball in honor of Julian, who had given him back his daughters.

The ballroom was lit with hundreds of candles and decorated with garlands of flowers from the palace garden. People came from far and wide, including the farmer who had raised Julian, Michael the cowherd and the village girl he was to marry, and Lady Mirabelle, who winked at Julian when she saw the pink laurel flower that he wore in the buttonhole of his black velvet suit.

When all the guests had arrived, the king rose to speak. His daughters and their suitors, including Jessamine and Julian, stood facing him in the front of the crowd. The princesses were dressed in their finest gowns and had never looked lovelier. "This man," he said, gesturing at Julian, "has given me back the greatest joy in my life: my daughters. For this, I owe him eternal gratitude. I also owe him the hand in marriage of one of these twelve beautiful women. Sir," he finished, facing Julian, "you may now choose among them."

Julian stepped forward, bowing. "If you please," he said to the king, "I have already made my choice."

"And I, mine," said Jessamine, stepping forward to join Julian.

The king beamed. "And so you shall marry," he said, "and be king and queen after me."

"Thank you," said Julian. "We will marry, but not just yet. We are young, and Jessamine is only now awake enough to truly enjoy life. In a few years, when we tire of swinging on the swing and playing amid the posies, we will become man and wife."

"Well said!" The king clapped his hands and laughed.

And the dancing began. Soon after the musicians struck up a tune, the king's eyes fell on Lady Mirabelle. From that moment on, he barely glanced at anyone else. She, too, had eyes only for him. They danced all evening together, as did the princesses and their suitors. Laughter and love filled the great ballroom that night and filled the king's palace forever after.

And in the garden, two sturdy laurel trees bloomed in every season, one with white blossoms and the other with blossoms of pink.